For Levi and Romeo,
Be whoever you are

And for Danielle,
Who let me be me

You're the loves of my life

Barker's Wish

Written by Dan Stern
Illustrated by Iva Žugić

And then one day he came upon
a cat crouched in the park.

Barker greeted her so sweet
with a smile and a...

The cat stood tall and smiled wide
and said with such a spark,

"Hello and greetings, hiya there,"
but it sounded like a...

Bark!

Barker and his new friend

made their voices
loud and pure.

And happy laughter from
their mouths